D1281576

More Advance Praise for
Pigeonholed in the
Land of Penguins

"They've done it again! A delightful and enduring homily that inspires us to open our eyes to new possibilities, both for ourselves and others. Full of insight and practical suggestions."

> —Barry Posner, Ph.D., co-author of *The Leadership Challenge*
> and Dean and Professor of Leadership at Santa Clara University

"The journey to self-awareness and interpersonal effectiveness is never-ending. From this charming, insightful book, I came to reconsider the question of who "they" are. Perhaps there is no "they?" There is only "we.""

> —Jim Schaffer, former CEO and President, Guy Gannett Communications
> and former President, *Chicago Sun Times*

"Too often we make assumptions that limit our view of what others can accomplish. *Pigeonholed in the Land of Penguins* helps us see what the results are. This book is a powerful teaching tool—great for team building, supervision, change management, and diversity workshops—just to name a few."

> —Julie O'Mara, co-author of *Managing Workforce 2000: Gaining
> the Diversity Advantage,* and President, O'Mara and Associates

"A practical, insightful, and important contribution to the discussion of personal and group productivity in the midst of increased diversity. The second part of the book, a primer on stereotyping, is particularly helpful."

> —James E. Hilvert, Executive Director,
> National Conference for Community and Justice

"BJ Hateley and Warren Schmidt challenge every manager to transcend organizational and occupational stereotypes. It is only by breaking down these preconceived notions that companies can tap into the latent talent, skill, and creativity of all their employees. In today's highly competitive marketplace, only those organizations that release their people from any and all types of pigeonholes will be successful."
—Man Jit Singh, CEO and President, FutureStep

"Another milestone in understanding diversity. This book expresses so clearly how pigeonholing limits people and organizations. It provides very useful, practical insights and tips for changing this self-defeating behavior."
—David W. Jamieson, Ph.D., co-author of
Managing Workforce 2000: Gaining the Diversity Advantage

"*Pigeonholed in the Land of Penguins* is a wake-up call. At a time when a diverse team will be the competitive advantage for the 21st-century organization, it is an innovative individual and group communications "system" that can help you and your organization reach new heights of success through your greatest assets—the people."
—Debbe Kennedy, author of *Diversity Breakthrough!*
founder and President of Leadership Solutions Companies

"This book is a 'must-read' for anyone, regardless of organizational level, who is interested in going beyond stereotypical thinking. Once again, Hateley and Schmidt have taken a complex issue and made it understandable and entertaining."
—Lenora Billings-Harris, author of
The Diversity Advantage: A Guide to Making Diversity Work

"*Pigeonholed in the Land of Penguins* is a quick and easy read for managers, supervisors, and all members of any organization. It provides illumination on issues of diversity, organizational behavior, and the thought processes of all of us as individuals."
—David J. Gascon, Deputy Chief of Police, Los Angeles Police Department

"*Pigeonholed in the Land of Penguins* teaches smart birds, by means of colorful imagery woven into a wise fable, the human skills and values they will need if their flocks are to fly high and far in the coming century."
—Willard Colston, Vice President of Strategy, Gemstar Development Corp.

PIGEONHOLED IN THE LAND OF PENGUINS

A Tale of Seeing beyond Stereotypes

Barbara "BJ" Hateley
Warren H. Schmidt

Illustrations by Sam Weiss

Missouri Western State College
Hearnes Learning Resources Center
4525 Downs Drive
St. Joseph, MO 64507

AMACOM
American Management Association
New York • Atlanta • Boston • Chicago • Kansas City • San Francisco • Washington, D.C.
Brussels • Mexico City • Tokyo • Toronto

Special discounts on bulk quantities of AMACOM books are available to corporations, professional associations, and other organizations. For details, contact Special Sales Department, AMACOM, a division of American Management Association, 1601 Broadway, New York, NY 10019.
Tel.: 212-903-8316   Fax: 212-903-8083
Web site: www.amanet.com

This publication is designed to provide accurate and authoritative information in regard to the subject matter covered. It is sold with the understanding that the publisher is not engaged in rendering legal, accounting, or other professional service. If legal advice or other expert assistance is required, the services of a competent professional person should be sought.

Library of Congress Cataloging-in-Publication data has been applied for and is on record at the Library of Congress.

© 2000 Barbara "BJ" Hateley.
All rights reserved.
Printed in the United States of America.

This publication may not be reproduced,
stored in a retrieval system,
or transmitted in whole or in part,
in any form or by any means, electronic,
mechanical, photocopying, recording, or otherwise,
without the prior written permission of AMACOM,
a division of American Management Association,
1601 Broadway, New York, NY 10019.

Printing number

10 9 8 7 6 5 4 3 2 1

We dedicate this book to all those
who yearn to fly free and show their true colors.

Foreword

Stories are powerful. The stories that we tell one another contain much insight and wisdom about what we believe and who we are as human beings. People learn from stories. Stories teach; stories inspire; stories provide food for the spirit as well as the mind. It is no accident that the Bible is written in stories, or parables. Classic fairy tales are stories that teach values and virtues to the young. Ancient myths are stories that create wisdom traditions, shaping civilizations for thousands of years.

I have always loved stories that both inspire and teach. People who know me can tell you how often I use stories in my own conversations, in my speeches, and in my daily life. I love to write great stories, and I love to *read* great stories.

Pigeonholed in the Land of Penguins is just the kind of story I love to read. It's a special story that captures the essence of a serious challenge — a challenge for organizations and for individuals. It's the problem of "pigeonholing" — stereotyping. When we pigeonhole people, we define them too narrowly and often overlook many aspects of their personalities, backgrounds, skills, and talents — to the detriment of both them and our organization.

Worse yet, we often pigeonhole ourselves — putting ourselves into confining boxes or categories, and then acting as if those categories are true, now and forever! Self-limiting beliefs are the worst form of pigeonholing. Because of them, we cheat ourselves and others of new experiences, challenging opportunities, and the fulfillment of our undeveloped potential.

Pigeonholed in the Land of Penguins picks up the story begun in the classic best-seller *A Peacock in the Land of Penguins,* a number of years later. Perry the Peacock and his friends have long since departed for the Land of Opportunity. But other new birds, including Paula and Pat, a pair of pigeons, have continued to struggle for acknowledgment and success in the Land of Penguins.

The Land of Penguins has a serious challenge to deal with — the challenge of change and declining resources. The pigeons think they have found a solution, but getting the attention of senior management is another matter! At the same time, other birds in the Land of Penguins are also struggling to be heard and seen for the talented, multifaceted individuals that they are. They resist being conveniently put into pigeonholes. As their story unfolds, the price of pigeonholing becomes apparent to one and all.

The first part of this book is the parable, a fable about stereotyping. The second part helps us all think about how to deal with the problem of stereotyping in our *own* lives and organizations. Together, these two parts give us both inspiration and practical advice.

Stories stick with people. And just as fine silverware gets a warm patina the more it is used, a fine story gets richer and warmer the more it is told and retold. It is my hope that this story will be told and retold many times in the years to come — and that like a classic fable, Bible story, or ancient myth, this story will illustrate, enlighten, entertain, and inspire all who read it and all who hear it. The authors' message is priceless!

— Ken Blanchard

Acknowledgments

This book is the sweet fruit that grows on the abundant tree of collaboration. Many people have contributed their thoughts and ideas to this story, and we are grateful to them all.

Chief among these are the creative spirits at CRM Films: Denise Dexter, Kirby Timmons, and Leslie Rodier, as well as Peter Jordan, Kym McQuisten, and Lyndi Calder — all of whom shared their ideas with us in the early inception of this project, and throughout the writing of the book and production of the video version of our story.

Our editor, Bill Hicks, is a kindred spirit who soars with us on our flights of creativity. His support, encouragement, and skillful editing helped turn this book from a dream into a reality.

Joel Marks of corVision Media, a dear, wonderful friend, also provided thoughtful critiques and creative suggestions in reaction to our original story treatment.

Our especially fabulous friend Ken Blanchard has been a role model and inspiration to us in all of our writing and publishing ventures, beginning with our original "Peacock story." We are *raving fans* who are *gung ho* about Ken!

Finally, and most important, our families provide the ongoing love and care that nurtures our hearts, feeds our minds, and lifts our spirits. We acknowledge the loving contributions of Michael Hateley, Reggie Schmidt, and Marjorie Weiss.

Our friends and family sometimes think we are "for the birds"
with all these penguin stories we write —
but they love us anyway!

To *all* of you we say:
Thank you. We love you. And we couldn't do it without you!

PART ONE

Once upon a time,
    in the not-so-distant past,
the Land of Penguins
was thriving
in the Sea of Organizations.

Resources were plentiful,
    and business was good.

They had come a long way
    since their early beginnings.

Once the exclusive domain
of penguins . . .

the Land had become increasingly diverse,
as birds of many kinds
came to make their home there —

    working hard
    to earn their place in the sun.

The penguins had come to see
the talent and skill
of these new birds
as important to the future
of their Land.

They even rewarded a few
of the new birds
for their achievements —
    by promoting them
    to leadership positions.

One day,
a bright young hawk named Harry
came to work in the Land of Penguins.

Palmer the Penguin
showed him around,
      giving him an orientation
      to his turf and terrain.

"Welcome to the Land of Penguins, Harry!"
      Palmer beamed.
"We're so happy to have you join us.
Let me show you where you'll be working ."

Palmer walked Harry down
      to the Sales office.

Harry was ever so polite,
wanting to make a good impression.
"I really appreciate
your arranging my orientation.
I plan to work hard
to show you what I can contribute."

He hesitated for a moment,
then continued haltingly,
"You know, I have a mechanical background.
Uh, perhaps I could . . .
Er, do you have any openings
in Engineering?"

Palmer Penguin
completely missed
Harry's hint:
> "Oh, I'm sure you'll be happy
> here in our Sales office, Harry."

Palmer smiled
as he patted
Harry on the back,
> "All the hawks who work here
> have done well."

Harry tried to continue,
> "Yes, but . . . ."

However, Palmer kept right on. . . .

"I'll check back with you later
to see how you're doing.

"In the meantime,
let me introduce you
to your supervisor,
Helen the Hawk.
　　　She'll show you the ropes."

Helen smiled at Harry
as Palmer waddled out the door.

"Come meet some of the others,"
    Helen reassured Harry
    as she guided him
    in the direction of a group of hawks.

Palmer Penguin
headed down the hall
toward the executive conference room
for a meeting
with some of the other penguins.

On his way,
he passed President Peter Penguin
and his son, Peter Jr.

Palmer couldn't help but overhear
bits and pieces
of their conversation.

President Peter was gesturing expansively
as he spoke.

"Someday, son, all this will be yours.
We've had a long, illustrious tradition of penguins
at the head of this organization,
    and I have every confidence
    that you'll carry on our proud heritage."

Peter Jr. protested in dismay,
"We've talked about this before, Dad.
I really want to be a designer!"

"Nonsense!"
      his father boomed.
"Penguins are born leaders!
Just forget your crazy idea
of becoming a designer —
that's for swans.
No son of mine
is going to work with swans!"

And with that,
      Peter Sr. turned on his heel
            and stormed back to his office.

"What on earth
has gotten into that young penguin of mine?"
he muttered to himself
as he arrived at his office door.

As he strode to his desk,
he noticed that the door to the conference room
adjoining his office
was closed.

Hearing muffled murmuring
on the other side,
he opened the door
to find a group of VIPs
(Very Important Penguins)
gathered around the conference table
with worried looks on their faces.

"What's the matter?"
President Peter asked.
"What's going on?"

The Very Important Penguins
glanced at one another.

Then Putney Penguin spoke up:
 "Well, sir,
 we've just gotten
 the latest production reports
 and we're concerned.
 We've seen a marked decrease
 in resources lately. . . .
 It's getting harder and harder
 to produce results."

Penny Penguin
nodded in agreement:
    "Something is happening
    in the Sea of Organizations,
        but no one seems to know what it is."

Just then, a pair of pigeons
appeared unexpectedly
in the doorway
to the conference room.

They were excited and eager
to share their news.

"Excuse us,
President Peter,
but we couldn't help overhearing
your conversation . . . ,"
        Paula the Pigeon began.

"Pat and I
have been doing some research,
and we found something
on the Internet
that could be the solution
to our problem.

Here, take a look at this printout. . . ."

President Peter was in no mood
for interruptions.

"Thank you, Paula,"
        he replied curtly.
"I appreciate your desire to help,
but we're very busy here.

"Just leave the printout
on my desk,
        and we'll schedule
        a meeting with you
        for another time."

Pat the Pigeon
tried to get their attention:

"Perhaps if we could tell you
a little more about it. . . .
 It's a contraption that will . . . ."

"That won't be necessary,"
Peter Penguin snapped.
"Now, if you will excuse us . . . ."

Paula and Pat
looked at each other.

Realizing that
they'd been brushed off
by the penguins,
    they put the printout
      on President Peter's desk
        and left the room.

As they closed the door behind them,
the pigeons overheard the penguins
resuming their discussion:

"Those *pigeons!* What were they thinking . . . ?
Barging into our meeting like that!"

Palmer Penguin snorted in exasperation.

"I'm certain they *meant* well . . .
but *really* now!"

Putney Penguin sniffed with disdain.

The other penguins chimed in. . . .

"They may be good
at scouting out information,
but, well, you know . . . ,"
    one began.

"Oh, I don't know.
Maybe they've got something
we should listen to,"
    one dissented.

"Get serious . . . ,"
    scoffed a third.

"You must be kidding . . . ,"
    echoed an incredulous fourth.

The pigeons walked dejectedly
down the hall.

Paula was visibly upset.

"I can't believe it!
They wouldn't even give us
a minute of their time,
        and we had something
        that could really *help!*"

Pat sighed in resignation.

"I was afraid that would happen.
It's dangerous to stick your neck out,
especially these days —
        everybody's so worried about the future.
        Just be glad you've got a job."

As time went on,
    things got worse
        in the Land of Penguins.

Productivity continued to decline
    as resources got scarcer and scarcer.

The penguins held meeting after meeting,
    but nothing seemed to help.

One day,
Paula and Pat
were out together
on a scouting expedition. . . .

Still smarting from the penguins' rebuff,
Paula grumbled to Pat:

  "We still haven't heard anything
  about rescheduling
  with President Penguin . . . .
  He's always tied up in meetings,
     and things keep getting worse and worse.
  Maybe we should call his office. . . ."

Pat shook his head vehemently:
"Nah, forget it . . . .
Those penguins don't want to hear from us.
After all, we're just pigeons."

Finally one day,
   President Penguin came across the printout
      the pigeons had left on his desk.

"Huh! I'd forgotten all about this!"
   he mumbled to himself
   as he read it.
"This might enable us
   to search for new resources.
Hmmm, maybe we should give it a try. . . ."

He called the head Purchasing Penguin
and told him
to place the order
that very same day.

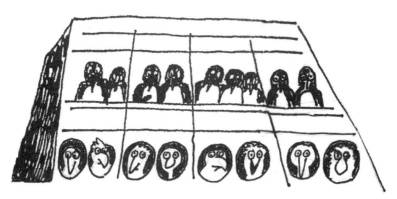

The penguins anxiously awaited
the arrival of their new contraption.

They waited and waited . . . .

Days turned into weeks,
  and weeks rolled into months.

Everyone wondered
  when it would arrive.

Finally,
  the contraption they had ordered,
    packed in a huge crate,
      was on its way . . . .

But alas,
the ship carrying their crate
got caught in a tremendous storm.

The crate
was swept overboard . . .

tossed about in the stormy sea . . .

. . . and finally washed up
on the shores of the Land of Penguins.

The penguins and a number of other birds
flew out of their offices
and gathered around
the jumble of pieces
lying on the shore.

To the birds' dismay,
the assembly instructions had been lost,
and there was no operating manual.

President Peter Penguin shook his head
as he surveyed the scene.

"What a mess . . . ," he clucked.
"How are we ever
going to put
this thing together?"

Edward the Eagle approached his boss.

"President Peter, sir . . . .

This looks like a job
for us eagles
in Engineering."

"Yes, of course,"
President Penguin agreed.

"How soon can
you have it completed?"

Edward pulled out his calculator.

"Well,
it's important
to approach these things
systematically."
   he replied.

"First we'll have to
draw up some plans . . . .

   "Then we'll have to
   double-check
   our specifications . . . .

      "Uh . . .
      we'll go to work on this
      right away . . . .

      "We'll get back to you
      as soon as we have
      something concrete
      to show you."

Edward and
the other eagles
retreated to
their drawing boards . . .

   . . . as the penguins
      looked quizzically
      at President Peter.

"So,
what are we supposed to do?"
      Penny Penguin asked plaintively.
"Just sit around and wait?!"

"Absolutely not!"
      President Peter replied.
"Time is of the essence!"

"Helen, I'm putting *your* team to work on this.
You hawks are great at producing results,
    even in tough situations.
I'm confident that
    you can solve this problem for us."

Helen puffed up her feathers
with pride as she turned
to her team . . . .

But just then,
Harry the Hawk cleared his throat,
trying to get Helen's attention:
   "*Ahem . . . Helen?*"

Helen glanced at him.
"Yes, Harry, what is it?"

"Uh, don't you think
we should wait
for Edward and the eagles?"
   Harry replied.
"They'll probably have
some good ideas."

Helen sniffed
    as she cut him off:

"Forget about those eagles
in Engineering . . . .
They'll just bury us in blueprints!
This is a job for *doers,*
    not *planners!*

"Besides, the boss gave *us* the job!"

And with that,
    she signaled the hawks
        to get to work.

The hawks
tore into the task
with their usual
energy and enthusiasm . . . .

But they were soon
arguing among themselves,
fighting for control,
and losing sight of their goal.

The pigeons
watched in dismay
as the chaos among the hawks
escalated.

Their squawking
and screeching
quickly turned into
clawing and biting.

Paula looked at Pat
and whispered to him,
  "Maybe we should offer to help . . . ?"

Pat immediately
shushed his friend:
  "No!
  I don't want to get brushed off again.
  especially by those hawks!"

Paula thought for a second,
then nodded her agreement.
  "Well, maybe you're right."

Pat continued,
self-doubt overcoming him,
  "Besides,
  if the hawks can't do it,
    what makes you think
    we can?"

The pigeons fell into frustrated silence.

President Peter Penguin was not so reluctant
to express *his* disappointment.
He shook his head
as he surveyed the scene:

"Those hawks are usually so capable —
I can't understand
    what went wrong here."

Putney Penguin,
trying to be helpful,
offered a suggestion:

"Maybe we need
to get some birds
who are gentler
and more cooperative
to work on this."

The penguins
turned to assess
the other birds
gathered on the shore.

"How about
the swans . . . ?"
   they all spoke at once.

" . . .They'll be perfect!"

Peter Penguin Jr.
brightened immediately.

"Oh, great!"
　　he exclaimed
"I've always wanted to work in design.
　　　This is my chance!
　I'll work *with* them!"

"Absolutely not!"
  Peter Sr. shouted.
"You are a penguin,
  not a swan!
Stay where you belong!"

Peter Jr. was crestfallen.
  "But, Dad . . ."
  he whined.

"I'll have none of it!"
  Peter Sr. harrumphed.

Peter Jr. slumped
  dejectedly.

Meanwhile, the swans
had quietly begun
to approach their task.

They were delighted
to be honored with the project.

Sara the Swan
whispered knowingly
to Sam the Swan,
  "You saw what happened
  when they put a bunch
  of those hawks together. . . ."

Sam nodded smugly,
  "We'll sort this out.
  We know how to work
  together."

But the swans had their *own* problems. . . .

As they gathered together
to begin working,
they were thoughtful
and ever so polite
to one another.

"After you, dear,"
        one would say.

"No, you go right ahead.
I insist,"
        another replied.

Fearful of seeming
rude or bossy,
they hung back
from their task.

They were so accustomed
to deferring to others
that no one
would take charge.

As a result . . .

. . . they were making
no progress at all.

Still watching
from the sidelines,
Paula the Pigeon shook her head
in exasperation.

She leaned over to Pat
and whispered,
  "Those swans
  are going nowhere with this.
    Maybe *now*
    we should offer to help."

Pat, still uncertain,
whispered back,
  "I dunno . . . .
  You can if you want to . . .
    but I'm staying out of this."

Paula decided
    to take a chance.

Mustering all the self-confidence she could,
she flew over to where
President Peter stood
with the other penguins.

"Excuse me, sir,"
    she began quietly.
"In that printout
we got off the Internet,
it said that . . . . "

"Look, Paula,"
    he interrupted,
"you pigeons have done your part.

"Don't worry —
    we've got everything under control."

Paula just stood there for a second,
    embarrassed in front of the others.

Then she quickly retreated
    to her friend Pat.

"See?"
      Pat hissed in her ear.
"I *told* you!
Getting involved in stuff
that's not your job
just gets you in trouble.
We should just keep quiet."

      Paula nodded silently,
still blushing from her rebuke.

The penguins conferred among themselves.

They looked
at the other birds,
    trying to figure out
    who should tackle
    the problem next.

Suddenly, the parrots
caught the penguins' attention.

"*We're* the best birds
to handle this problem!" the parrots squawked.

"*We're* the creative ones!
"Give *us* a crack at it!"

The penguins thought a moment,
then quickly agreed:

"Yes, yes,"
        they replied
"You'll do a great job!
But get busy on it!
        We've wasted too much time already!"

The parrots were thrilled:
        "We'll have this contraption together
        in a wink!"

And with that,
   the parrots all jumped in,
      screeching and squawking,
         flashing their colorful feathers,
   creating a jumble
      of creative excitement.

Feathers,
   feet,
   heads,
   and tails
   were flying every which-way!

But while most of the parrots
were thrashing about,
one of them
stood quietly by,
deep in thought,
watching the others.

"C'mon, get busy, Pam,"
    the parrots shrilled at her.

"What's the matter with you?"

But Pam the Parrot
would not budge.

"I don't think
we should be so impulsive,"
        she replied.

"I think we should take
a more logical, analytical approach.
We need to step back
and take a look
at the big picture
before jumping into the action."

The other parrots hooted at her in disdain:

"Ridiculous!"

"What's with you, anyway?"

"You sound like one
of those pigeons!"

"C'mon,
       get with the program!"

And they kept right on . . .

       . . . thrashing about . . .

              . . . in their creative chaos.

Finally,
when the dust settled
and the parrots stepped back . . .

all birds fell into stunned silence.

They could hardly believe
what was before their eyes.

The parrots' imaginative contraption
was a sight to behold . . .

    but no one could see
    what on earth
    it might be good for!

"Uh . . . well, it's *different,*"
    Peter Jr. said,
        trying to be polite.

The parrots were proud of their creation —
    and surprised
        that no one praised them
            for their imagination
                and ingenuity.

At this point,
the pigeons
    were about ready
    to jump out of their feathers!

Paula, in particular,
    could no longer contain herself.

She jumped forward, shouting:

    "I've *had* it!
    I've got to *do* something!"

As the startled birds turned to look at her,
she continued,
    "You know, if everyone would just . . . ."

This time,
it was Palmer Penguin
who cut her off:
    "Paula! Now you just step aside.
    We'll handle this."

Pat grabbed Paula's wing
and pulled her away
from the group once again,
whispering in her ear,
    "When will you learn?
    Just keep your mouth shut
    and stay out of trouble!"

Putney Penguin
didn't bother to hide his disgust
with the whole situation.

"Just look at this mess!"
        he exclaimed.
"We never should have delegated
this to those *other* birds!
Clearly, this is a job for *executives!*"

President Peter nodded sagely:

"You're absolutely right.
We should have handled this ourselves
        from the beginning.

What this situation calls for is *leadership!*"

The other penguins
nodded in unison.

As if on a signal,
they stepped forward
en masse
and attempted
    to assemble
        the contraption themselves.

They looked so dignified
in their stark black and white.
    waddling to and fro,
        back and forth,
            pecking and poking.

But alas,
they ended up
in less-than-
dignified
failure.

President Penguin
blustered and flustered
in embarrassment:

"Well, there *must* be a piece missing!
That's the problem."

Paula the Pigeon,
who had been watching with Pat,
took a deep breath,
        then stepped forward
        one more time.

"You know,
there's another way
to approach this . . . ."

Again,
Palmer Penguin snapped at her,
   "Why do you keep interrupting?
      What *is* it?"

Paula's friend Pat rolled his eyes
and muttered to himself:

"Oh boy, *now* she's gonna get it!"

All the penguins glared at Paula.

But Paula bravely continued,
    "Well, we . . .
    I mean, well . . .
    while all of you were busy
    trying to sort this out,
        we pigeons were talking . . . ."

Pat looked away
    as he mumbled,
"Leave me outta this . . . ."

Paula didn't miss a beat:

"Maybe instead
of each group of birds
working on the problem
by themselves . . .

. . . we should pick birds
who have good ideas
regardless of who they are,
or which department
they come from."

"That's a crazy idea!"
   President Peter Penguin snorted.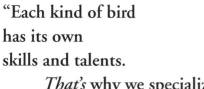

"Everybody knows
that we should each do
what we do best.

"Each kind of bird
has its own
skills and talents.
   That's why we specialize."

Harry the Hawk
　　saw an opening
　　　　and jumped into the debate:

　　　　"But some of us
　　　　see things *differently*
　　　　from others
　　　　in our own departments.
　　　　　We're not all alike,
　　　　　you know."

At which point,
Peter Penguin Jr.
chimed in:

"See, Dad?
      It's not just me.
I have more in common
                  with the swans
                        than with the other penguins."

Pam the Parrot
joined the chorus:

"And I keep trying
to tell the other parrots
that we need to think
more like the pigeons . . .
    . . . you know, not so impulsive."

Palmer Penguin looked stunned and confused.

"But, but . . . ."
    he stammered,
"everybody knows
that birds of a feather
should flock *together."*

Putney Penguin sided with Palmer:
    "Besides,
    we've never done anything
    like this before.
        It'll never work."

But Peter Penguin Jr.
wouldn't give up.

"Well,
that 'birds of a feather' notion
hasn't worked.
Why not give
Paula's idea a chance?
　　How about letting
　　some of us do things
　　a *different* way?

　　　"... What do we have to lose?"

By this time,
most of the other birds
were beginning
to agree . . .

some wholeheartedly . . .

some with reservations.

The penguins
finally relented.

"OK,"
President Peter
said resignedly.
"Go ahead."

The birds immediately set to work.

Paula the Pigeon,
along with Harry the Hawk,
Sara the Swan,
Peter Penguin Jr.,
and Pam the Parrot,
as well as several other birds,
    all joined in.

Each of them
brought their own
unique skills and talents
to the task,
  sharing ideas
    and learning from
      one another.

Paula the Pigeon provided
valuable information
and insight
    as the group set about
    its appointed task.

Her background in research
made her a key resource
for group learning.

Harry the Hawk was finally able
to demonstrate the mechanical abilities
he had been longing to use.

He helped the birds
organize their work
in a methodical, practical way.

Sara the Swan took on
a leadership role,
  skillfully guiding
  and coaching the birds
  as they went about their task.

Her ability
to bring out the best in others
  enabled them all to
  work together productively.

Pam the Parrot,
with her thoughtful analysis
and her eye for detail,
>made sure the birds were thorough,
>not leaving anything to chance.

Peter Penguin Jr. used his design skills
and his artistic flair
to think creatively
about the task at hand.

He inspired his teammates
to think "outside the box"
and not be limited
by their past
experience.

Each of the other birds
who worked on the team
        brought their own
        unique abilities
        to bear on the project.

They did not limit themselves
with assumptions
        based on
        style or status.

Rather,
they decided
who should do what,
        based on talent and skill.

They saw each bird as an individual,
with his or her own special set of
    ideas,
        experience,
            skills,
                and abilities

(none of which had anything to do
with the color of their feathers
or their traditional job descriptions).

They worked together quickly —
sorting and sifting,
  building and bolting,
    crafting and constructing.

The penguins watched and waited, —
by turns skeptical and curious.

Could they do it?
Would they be successful?

Everything was riding
on this varied flock of birds —
  working together in a new way —
    with only their good will
    and good sense
    to guide them.

Finally,
the birds stepped back.

The contraption was complete.

The birds gaped in amazement

at what they had created —

an *incredible undersea explorer!*

Admiring their handiwork,
Paula explained
    to the other birds:

"Now we can go
    anywhere we want
        in the Sea of Organizations . . .

   " . . . seeking out more resources
        and new opportunities."

The penguins
looked at each other . . .

then they looked
at the pigeons.

President Peter Penguin
broke the silence:

"And to think,
we almost
lost out
simply because
we didn't see
the skills and talents we have among us.
Our own shortsightedness
almost cost us
this great new machine!"

All the birds
    began to look at each other
        with new eyes.

They saw how they had *all* been blinded
    by their stereotypes of one another.

Now . . .
    they were beginning to appreciate
    the *uniqueness* of each bird.

They saw for the first time
    how they were different,
        as well as how they were similar!

It was clear to them,
as never before,
    that appearances can be deceiving —
        and things are not always what they seem.

The birds had learned
three very important things . . .

1.   Don't judge a bird
     by its feathers.

     *(Good ideas often come
     from the most unlikely sources.)*

2.   Birds of *different* feathers
    can flock together!

*(When individual differences
are valued and appreciated,
the team is more likely
to create breakthroughs in
   innovation
      and
        productivity.)*

3. And,
  most important,
    we must *always*
      guard against
        pigeonholing each other . . .

 and pigeonholing *ourselves* as well!

(When we are self-aware
and honestly examine our motives,
we can free others —
as well as ourselves —
from the stifling limits of stereotypes.)

The birds were humbled
by what they had learned
    and they were also grateful.

They knew that their world was changing
    and that new challenges
    and new obstacles
        lay before them.

Mustering their courage,
they climbed aboard
their undersea explorer
and headed out
into the Sea of Organizations.

Currents were shifting,
both East and West,
and with each changing tide
came new dangers
and new opportunities.

As they moved ahead
into the vast unknown
of the Future . . .

all the birds kept their eyes open . . .

    everyone watching
       for new possibilities,

and sharing their ideas about new opportunities.

Perhaps
most important of all . . .

they now realized
that the resources they were seeking
far and wide

    paled in comparison

      to the resources
      they had discovered
        within themselves.

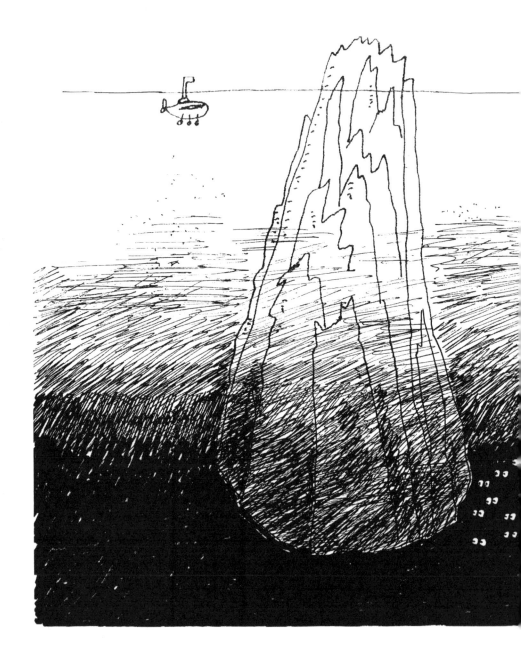

THE END

(or could it be just the beginning . . . ?)

PART TWO

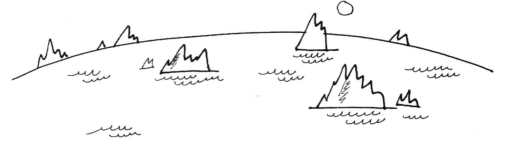

From Parable to Practice

The birds' adventure in the Land of Penguins is just the proverbial "tip of the iceberg." Stereotypes are stubbornly persistent, both in individuals and in organizations. Like icebergs, stereotypes are largely hidden deep in our subconscious minds, subtly influencing our interactions with one another. And like the *Titanic*, some of our loftiest goals and noblest intentions are often wrecked by these icebergs.

Navigating successfully through these hazards and other dangers in the Sea of Organizations requires vigilant self-awareness, compassionate honesty, and a willingness to look at people and situations in an open, unbiased way. The following pages are designed to help you spot limiting assumptions within yourself and break out of the "penguin suit" of narrow-minded thinking.

Whether you read these pages by yourself or study them in seminar situations, the key factor is a willingness to look deeply and honestly at your own thinking and behavior.

It is our hope that the tips, strategies, checklists, and guidelines here will help you to free yourself — and your organization — from the destructiveness of stereotypes and pigeonholes.

We send you our best wishes as you explore the uncharted territory of the future!

Additional Resources for Liberating People from Pigeonholes

Key Learning Points from the Story

1. Our tendency to prefer others like ourselves, and our assumption that some groups are superior to others, may cause us to exclude those who have an important contribution to make.

2. When we can overcome our biases and egos, we free others to make their fullest contributions.

3. Good ideas often come from the most unlikely sources.

4. Our strengths (aggressiveness, politeness, creativity, etc.) can also become weaknesses when we overdo them.

5. There is always some danger to be aware of and concerned about (e.g., changing market conditions, declining resources, etc.), both for individuals and for organizations.

6. There are often unexpected challenges that provide new opportunities (for instance, the machine arrives with no instructions).

7. The key tasks of any organization are:
   - To identify new potential opportunities
   - To understand them and explore how best to exploit them to benefit the organization
   - To bring the experience and brainpower of the people in the organization to bear on the opportunities

8. These are some potential blocks to this process:
   - Seeing only parts of the problem or solution (e.g. focusing on pieces of machinery rather than the entire apparatus).
   - Limiting our explorations and discussions to those we feel most comfortable with — those who are most like ourselves.
   - Not asking "Who else might know something about this or have an interest in it?"
   - Ignoring or overlooking those who might have a special contribution, or even the key to the solution.

9. When we tap into the full creativity of everyone on a team, we open ourselves up to significant breakthroughs in innovation, productivity, and team effectiveness.

10. Leaders of organizations have the critical responsibility to seek out and recognize the talent available in their diverse workforce. It is essential that executives and managers serve as powerful role models for diverse teamwork in action.

A Few
Words about
Pigeonholes

The human mind thinks in categories — and we need these categories to help us organize all that we experience as we go through daily life. Without categories, our brains would be filled with a jumble of disconnected facts, impressions, sights, sounds, thoughts, ideas, sensations, etc. Our categories help us make sense of the world we live in and give us a shorthand way to respond to people and events.

The categories in our minds contain not just facts and data — they also contain meanings and evaluations. Our categories are usually not neutral. We usually have *feelings* about categories. These feelings may be positive or negative. Mention of a category often triggers an instant reaction, almost a reflex. For instance, note how you feel when the following words are mentioned to you:

Vegetables	Politicians	Rodents
Italians	Beaches	Dogs
Newspapers	Rock 'n' Roll	Engineers
Blondes	Attorneys	Immigrants
Athletes	Modern Art	Priests
Mercedes	Southerners	Factories

Notice that your reactions to these words may be positive, negative, or a mixture of both. But your reactions are rarely neutral. Most of us have judgments, opinions, and feelings about most categories of things. This is appropriate and normal.

While categories are not a problem in and of themselves, they become a problem when we cannot distinguish between the characteristics of a category and the characteristics of an individual item or person within that category. Put another way, the category turns into a stereotype when we can no longer see an individual tree but only the forest. When we assume that all trees within a forest are identical and cannot see that each individual tree has some characteristics in common with the others but is also unique in its own way — that is when our category turns into a stereotype.

We use the word *pigeonhole* for *stereotype* in our story. The dictionary defines a stereotype as "a fixed or conventional notion or conception, as of a person, group, idea, etc., held by a number of people, and allowing for no individuality, critical judgment, etc." *

We all understand that negative stereotypes are destructive and debilitating. But positive stereotypes are a problem too. "Even positive images deny a person's individuality, defining him (or her) by a set of spurious characteristics." **

The key problem with stereotypes is that they are fixed, unthinking, undiscerning, and limiting. Stereotypes limit the people to whom the stereotype is applied, and they limit the person doing the stereotyping as well. Everyone loses when stereotypes erase critical judgment. Individuals lose, and organizations lose as well.

* *Webster's New World Dictionary,* 1974.
** Randy Cohen, "A Novel Solution," *The New York Times,* May 9, 1999.

Quiz: Have You Ever Been Pigeonholed by Others?

☐ ☐ 1. Have other people been surprised when they learned something about you that didn't fit their image of you?

☐ ☐ 2. Have you felt like you or your ideas were not taken seriously because of some category into which others had put you?

☐ ☐ 3. Have you found yourself saying or doing things in such a way as to break out of other people's preconceived image of you?

☐ ☐ 4. Are you routinely excluded from certain activities because of assumptions that others make about you?

☐ ☐ 5. Have other people made comments about you based on your race, gender, age, physical appearance, religion, occupation, clothes, manner of speaking, and so on?

☐ ☐ 6. Do you sometimes feel frustrated because it seems that other people don't see you for who you really are?

☐ ☐ 7. Do other people have *positive* expectations of you, based on some category they have you in — expectations that you don't feel you can live up to?

☐ ☐ 8. When you first meet people, can you see that they are talking to you or responding to you in a certain way because of assumptions they have made about who you are?

☐ ☐ 9. Do you ever have to explain to people how they have miscategorized you?

☐ ☐ 10. Have you ever been singled out as a representative of a particular group (based on race, gender, age, occupation, etc.) and asked to speak for that group?

__ __ TOTALS

134

Scoring

If you marked "yes" on three items or fewer, you are incredibly fortunate! You have rarely been pigeonholed by others, and you feel that you are seen as an individual and appreciated for who you are as a person.

If you marked "yes" on four to seven items, you have had some significant experiences of being pigeonholed by others. You can certainly empathize with those who are pigeonholed all the time because you've been there many times yourself. But there are also times when you are able to break out of your pigeonhole and be seen as a unique individual.

If you marked "yes" on eight to ten items, you might as well feather your nest as best you can, because you're spending plenty of time there! You are constantly frustrated by other people's view of you and their corresponding behavior. You feel misunderstood and unappreciated for the range of talent and ability you feel you have to offer. You may even be feeling cynical and/or depressed because this pigeonholing happens to you so often.

What to Do if You Find Yourself Being Pigeonholed by Others

Pigeonholing is a fact of life. We all do it. We know only a small part of another human being's experience, skills, and motivation. We can't read other people's minds or know everything about their background and personal attributes. So we make educated guesses based on the little information we do have. We make assumptions and generalizations based on the data available to us. We all do it. It's human.

So we shouldn't be shocked when other people pigeonhole *us*! It may be frustrating; it may even be hurtful. And it's a fact of life in organizations as well as in society at large. When someone misjudges, misunderstands, or misperceives us, it is an experience to be understood and dealt with as constructively as possible.

Here are some questions to ask yourself when you suspect someone is pigeonholing you:

1. What does this person really know about me?
2. Why should I expect them to see me differently, given the little information they have about who I am and what my capabilities are?
3. What is their motivation in pigeonholing me? Is it simply out of ignorance or faulty assumptions, or is their behavior conscious, deliberate, and ill-intentioned?
4. What do I have to gain by trying to get this person to see me differently?
5. Do I have anything to *lose* by trying to get this person to see me differently?
6. Should I ask other people how to handle this situation with this person?
7. Am I choosing my battles wisely? Is this worth the effort?

8. How have I handled situations like this in the past? What strategies have been most effective for me?

9. How have other people handled situations when they are pigeonholed? What have I learned from watching others deal with pigeonholing?

10. What is my true goal and my true motivation in wanting to get out of this pigeonhole?

Here are some guidelines to think about as you consider what to do:

1. Avoid putting the other person on the defensive.

2. If you choose to have a conversation with the person, choose your time and place wisely. Do not embarrass them in front of others. Do not choose a time when they are distracted or tense.

3. Use "I" language, not "you" language (e.g., "I noticed that my idea was overlooked in the meeting this morning. I think I have some good contributions to make. Could you help me find ways to raise my ideas more effectively, so that others can see what I have to offer?"). Do not confront or accuse (e.g., "You never listen to my ideas."): That simply makes the other person defensive, and you'll get nowhere.

4. Ask for feedback from other people about how you are perceived in your department or organization. Chances are, others do not perceive you the way you perceive yourself.

5. Accept the fact that you are going to have to retrain others to see you differently. It will take time and effort to break out of the pigeonholes in which others may see you. Think carefully about the things you can do to appear different in the eyes of others.

6. Once labeled, it is very hard to change people's perceptions of you. Whenever you take a new job or work in a new orga-

nization, consider in advance the behavior, attire, attitude, and communication skills that you'll need to deliberately and consciously help other people see you the way you want to be seen.

7. Break out of pigeonholes by surprising people (in a positive way) with your knowledge, experience, skill, and talent. You may need to volunteer for special projects or take on extra responsibilities outside your job description. Doing this on a regular basis over time will help reshape the way others see you.

8. Talk to other people about your past job experience, your education, and your personal hobbies or activities. That will give them a broader perspective on who you are and what you have to contribute. Do so in an appropriate manner, of course.

9. Always be aware that *who you are being* often speaks louder than *what you are saying or doing*. If you are feeling resentful, angry, or superior and self-righteous, it is bound to show through, no matter how carefully you pick your words. Always be aware of your attitude and how it affects the way others perceive you.

10. Be patient; be forgiving; be gracious. We are all in this together and have to find ways to work and live together more effectively. Give the other person the benefit of the doubt. We live in very confusing times, with rapid change, new challenges to deal with, and an increasingly diverse group of people with whom we must interact. Cut the other person some slack, and they are more likely to do the same for you. Take life seriously, but take yourself lightly.

Quiz: Do You Ever Pigeonhole Yourself?

HOW OFTEN DO YOU THINK OR SAY:

	Never 1	Rarely 2	Sometimes 3	Often 4
1. It's no use trying. They won't listen to me anyway.	—	—	—	—
2. I don't have enough experience to do that job.	—	—	—	—
3. What do I know? I'm just a _____ (fill in the blank) _____.	—	—	—	—
4. I tried that once. It didn't work. I can't do it.	—	—	—	—
5. People like me can't ever get ahead here.	—	—	—	—
6. Every time I try something new, I fail.	—	—	—	—
7. My parents said I'd never amount to anything. They were right.	—	—	—	—
8. I'm not qualified. I don't have the right credentials.	—	—	—	—
9. If I take a risk and fail, my career here will be over.	—	—	—	—
10. I have a reputation to live up to.	—	—	—	—
11. It's important to know your place, pay your dues, and not rock the boat.	—	—	—	—
12. I wish I could, but I can't.	—	—	—	—
13. I've never done that before. I couldn't possibly do it.	—	—	—	—
14. It's important to fit in and be like everyone else. People don't like it if you're different.	—	—	—	—
15. It never pays to stick your neck out.	—	—	—	—

ADD UP YOUR TOTAL POINTS _____

Scoring

15–26 You spend little time in self-imposed pigeonholes. You see yourself as having lots of options and opportunity.

27–38 You are concerned about others' perceptions of you and sometimes limit yourself and your opportunities for the future.

39–49 You've created some significant pigeonholes for yourself and have put a lid on your ability to try new things and take risks.

50–60 You spend almost all your time cowering in the pigeonholes in your own mind. You place considerable emphasis on what other people think, or on what *you think they will think.*

Ways in Which We Stereotype Ourselves

Often, the ways we stereotype ourselves are even more limiting and destructive than the stereotyping we do to others! We do it in many subtle, and not-so-subtle ways:

1. We accept any critical or negative statement our parents or others made about us as true forever (e.g., "I'm a klutz," "I'm not creative," or "I'm not very smart").

2. We have one failure experience or one career setback, and we give up on any future opportunities (e.g., "I tried that once — it didn't work. I'm not doing *that* again!").

3. We compare ourselves to others and find ourselves inadequate (e.g., "Oh, I could never start my own business. I don't have your self-confidence").

4. We buy into common social stereotypes and apply them to ourselves (e.g., "I'm just a woman. . . . What do I know about being a leader?").

5. We let our fear of making mistakes and/or looking foolish keep us from taking risks that could help us grow, both personally and professionally (e.g., I could never get up in front of the group like that").

6. We second-guess and doubt our own ideas before we ever even share them with others or try them out (e.g., "Maybe I should just keep my mouth shut. It's probably a dumb idea anyway").

7. We rely too heavily on other people's opinions and advice about what we should do (e.g., "My parents and school counselors said I was good at math, so I went into accounting").

8. We made decisions about ourselves long ago, and have let those decisions keep us from testing our abilities in new areas (e.g., "I was always small for my age, so I never tried sports. I became a bookworm instead").

9. We too often choose perceived safety and security over the opportunity for risks and rewards, based on our own self-image (e.g., "I'll die if I lose this job, so I'll just play it safe, keep a low profile, and keep my mouth shut").

10. We assume that other people see us the way we see ourselves (e.g., "I'm just a worker bee. No one wants my opinion").

Ways in Which We Sterotype Others

Stereotypes are part and parcel of social and organizational life. Undoubtedly, *all* of us have made assumptions about other people based on partial or limited information and knowledge about them. Here are some of the many ways in which we succumb to stereotypes:

1. We assume things about another person based only on his or her occupation (e.g., "Typical salesman!").

2. We assume that everyone in a category is like everyone else in that category (e.g., "You know how those engineers are").

3. We assume that certain categories of people are naturally suited to certain activities or jobs (e.g., "Wow, you're tall. I'll bet you played basketball in high school," or "Women can have great careers in human resources or public relations").

4. We assume that certain professions are unsuitable or off-limits to whole categories of people (e.g., "Women can't be successful in tough, manufacturing environments").

5. We take some people's ideas and suggestions more seriously than others, based on their job classification or job grade level (e.g., "Well, he's the manager. He's in a position to know").

6. We discount information from some people, based on assumptions we make about their intelligence or creativity, which is in turn based on some category we put them in (e.g., "What does he know? He's only a clerk!").

7. We limit career advancement and job changes for others because we see them in a limited

way, suited for only one type of job or career (e.g., "She applied for a job in marketing? But she's always worked in human resources! She'll never make it").

8. We look only at a person's *past* experience, rather than considering their *future* potential. (e.g., "But he's never been a manager before").

9. We don't take the time to find out about the full range of a person's talent, skill, and experience. We don't get to know them (e.g., "How could she leave our company and go to work for a TV station? I didn't know she had any background in broadcasting").

10. We make assumptions based on a person's physical appearance, rather than learning about their abilities, skills, and interests (e.g., "She sure doesn't *look* like a CEO!").

11. We make assumptions about a person's work habits based on geographical stereotypes (e.g., "You know how intense and driven New Yorkers are," or "He's from South America. You know, he works on mañana time").

12. We attribute both positive and negative characteristics to people based on only one piece of information about them (e.g., "He's Japanese so he must be smart." "She's a professional athlete, so she must be lesbian," "He's a computer programmer, so he must be a geek," "He's a professor, so he must be absentminded," or "She's pretty, so she's not very smart").

Signs That You May Be Pigeonholing Others More Often than You Realize

Pigeonholing is such a common practice that we often slip into it without even realizing it. In our busy lives, we often make snap judgments about people based on very little information — often superficial information. It's not because we're bad people. It's because of all-too-human tendency that takes a terrific toll on both individuals and organizations. The costly results include overlooking important information, giving short shrift to people who have good contributions to make, missing out on valuable talent, and sending frustrating and hurtful implicit messages to people who might otherwise have become valuable friends and associates.

Here is a list of just some of the warning signs that suggest you might be pigeonholing others more often than you realize:

1. You don't listen attentively to someone because you have decided that a person like that doesn't really know much about the topic being discussed.

2. It never even occurs to you to ask someone for their ideas because of their job classification, department, gender, race, age, or other category in which you see them.

3. You get irritated when someone you perceive as having no expertise or credibility insists on trying to make a point.

4. When someone accuses you of having a closed mind about a certain person, you become defensive and resentful and try to justify your behavior.

5. You think you're a good judge of people, and you pride yourself on being able to size people up quickly.

6. You feel good when someone else gets "put in their place."

7. If someone you have sized up behaves in a way contrary to your expectations, you either discount their actions or make them an exception to the rule.

8. You don't engage certain people in conversations outside their clearly defined area of expertise. It never occurs to you that they might know a lot about many things outside their immediate job description.

9. You never consider certain individuals for job opportunities outside their present field. It doesn't occur to you that perhaps those people could do many different jobs and be effective.

10. You find yourself often referring to other people in terms of their occupation, job classification, skin color, accent, gender, country of origin, or some other category, rather than their personal attributes or characteristics.

Tips and Strategies for Reducing Our Own Tendency to Stereotype Others

1. Awareness and consciousness are the first steps toward changing any undesired behavior or attitude. Begin by simply being aware of the inner voices, opinions, and judgments you have about people. Ask yourself: *Am I really looking at this person as an individual, or I have I lumped them into a category with others who are like them?*

2. Try an experiment: Pick someone who is very different from you to have a conversation with. Tell yourself that everything you thought you knew about them is false. What questions would you ask that person to find out who they really are? What would be your attitude in listening if you genuinely want to learn about that person?

3. There are two ways to approach another person in conversation and interaction. One way is with an *intent to learn;* the other is with an *intent to protect.* With an intent to learn, you are open to hearing that person's ideas, perspectives, and feelings. With an intent to protect, you are closed to them, and your primary goal is to defend yourself, your feelings, or your beliefs. Practice approaching people more often with an

intent to learn, especially with people who are different from you. See if it enhances your relationships with others.

4. Learn to be a better listener. Most of us are good at talking and expressing our own ideas, feelings, and opinions. But many of us are not very good listeners. Take a class in effective listening skills, or read a book on listening. Practice often. The better you listen, the more you learn. What you learn may surprise you — and enhance your life!

5. We judge *ourselves* by our intentions, but we judge *others* by their behavior. We are quick to declare ourselves innocent of offense, by virtue of our good intentions. But we are quick to take offense at others' behavior, without giving them any credit at all for *their* good intentions. Give the other person the benefit of the doubt. We live in a time when diversity makes effective communication more challenging than ever. Virtually 80 percent of offensive remarks are unintentional, often based on ignorance, mistaken assumptions, and *unconscious* stereotyping, rather than maliciousness. An open, honest dialogue about hurt feelings or offended sensibilities will frequently clear up misunderstandings on both sides. Give others the same benefit of the doubt that you'd like them to give to you.

6. We tend to spend most of our time with people we feel most comfortable around — people like ourselves. This isn't bad. It's normal, and it's safe. But it also keeps us separate from others, and it keeps us from ever learning about those who are different. Spend more time with people who are different from you. Doing so will probably mean getting out of your "comfort zone." Overcoming stereotypes and learning to appreciate diversity means *getting comfortable with being uncomfortable.*

7. Any time we see another person as simply a member of a particular group, rather than as an individual within a group, we

are in danger of succumbing to stereotypes. Practice seeing others as individuals first, as group members second.

8. As Stephen Covey suggests, "Seek first to understand, then to be understood." Live and work with others with an attitude of respect, caring, and authenticity. Create a safe space in which others can discuss the problems of stereotyping with you. A community of people engaged in learning to see beyond stereotypes is much more powerful and effective than any one person alone. Encourage dialogue with others. Be aware of how "political correctness" can sometimes hinder open, honest communication about differences.

9. Recognize that overcoming the natural human tendency to stereotype is a never-ending process. Those years of cultural conditioning and socialization have given you hundreds, if not thousands, of stereotypes that do not serve you well. Begin now to root out those stereotypes, one by one. Like tending a garden and pulling weeds, tending your thoughts and attitudes is an ongoing process that requires persistence, patience, and vigilance. Weeding out stereotypes will result in a more fruitful "garden" of knowledge, insight, and relationships.

10. Celebrate your progress and personal successes in overcoming stereotypes. Learn from your mistakes and shortcomings.

Tips and Strategies for Reducing Sterotyping in Organizations

1. Management's attitude and behavior are critical elements in any organizational effort to overcome stereotypes. Executives, managers, and supervisors must constantly monitor their own language and behavior, for they are important role models for everyone else in the organization. People always pay more attention to what leaders *do*, rather than what they say. After all, actions speak louder than words. Whenever there is a gap between what leaders say and what they do, their credibility is seriously damaged. Leaders who do not "walk their talk" quickly become ineffective, and often become the laughingstock of employees.

2. Policies and procedures need to be thoroughly evaluated in terms of equity, fairness, and effectiveness, in light of workforce diversity. Stereotypes can get in the way of formulating guidelines and policies. Implicit values and judgments can inadvertently reinforce stereotypes in the organization.

3. Well-intentioned diversity training can sometimes backfire and simply reinforce damaging stereotypes. Whenever people are discussed only in terms of their membership in a particu-

lar group (gender, race, age, religion, culture, etc.), the risk is high that stereotypes are being perpetuated rather than dispelled. Whenever you hear people make broad, generalized statements about groups of people, be alert for potential stereotyping. (For instance, "Here's how to communicate with Native Americans." or, "Asians are all concerned about 'saving face'" or, "Women are _____ (fill in the blank) _____," or, "When supervising Generation X employees, remember that _____ (fill in the blank) _____," or, "Sales people are all extroverts"). Broad-brush generalizations about groups of people can very easily turn into stereotyping.

4. The old childhood taunt "sticks and stones will break my bones, but words can never hurt me" is patently false. Language is everything. We communicate meaning and values through language. We communicate who we are through language. We communicate who we think others are through language. Language shapes our perception, how we see the world around us. We understand ourselves and our work through language. In our organizations we must be ever conscious of our language and the effect it has on other people — coworkers, customers, vendors, bosses, employees, shareholders, clients, etc.

5. Try an experiment: Eliminate the word *they* from your organization's vocabulary for a set period of time (say, one month). Consider the possibility that there is only *we* — there is no *they*. See what this simple change in language does to how you and others think about solving problems, generating creative ideas, getting the work done, holding meetings, sending out memos, thinking about ownership, and fostering personal accountability and empowerment. If there is no *they*, there is only *we* and *us*. It changes everything.

6. Be wary of diversity initiatives that can be seen as superficial window-dressing. Sometimes, celebrating Black History Month, Cinco de Mayo, or other cultural events can backfire — as they are seen as reinforcing ethnic stereotypes and perpetuating racial divisions. They are also sometimes seen as an easy cop-out for management — a way of saying that diversity is appreciated, when there are still significant barriers (often subtle and insidious) to *truly* valuing diversity in the deepest sense.

7. One of the most effective ways to break down stereotypes is for diverse people to work together on projects with clearly defined goals and objectives. As people focus their attention on getting the job done, they start to learn more about their fellow teammates and learn that they had mistaken ideas about one another. The breakdown of stereotypes is a happy by-product of task-focused diverse work teams.

8. Everyone in the organization has a contribution to make in building an atmosphere of trust, respect, honor, honesty, openness, and authentic communication. It is not just the job of management. Every person can start by looking at his or her own attitude, communication, and behavior at work. Organizational change can be grass roots and bottom-up, just as well as it can be top-down. Don't wait for other people to change. Start with yourself.

9. Get everyone in the organization focused on reducing stereotypes as an important organizational goal. Help people see what's in it for them. Include customers, suppliers, and vendors, as well as managers and employees. Good ideas for positive organizational change can sometimes come from surprising places.

10. There are no quick fixes. Give up the search for magic bullets to fix your organization. Reducing stereotypes is an ongoing, never-ending process, requiring the commitment of all. Learn from your mistakes — and celebrate your successes!

Additional Materials

Additional Materials for Pigeons and Penguins are available from:

Peacock Productions
701 Danforth Drive, Los Angeles, CA 90065
Phone: 323-227-6205   fax: 323-227-0705
E-mail: PeacockHQ@aol.com
Web site: www.peacockproductions.com

Videos

"A Peacock in the Land of Penguins" (11 minutes)

This best-selling animated video has been a consistent hit with organizations of all types and sizes. It has achieved the status of "diversity classic" and is used in seminars, conferences, team meetings, and training sessions. The story deals not only with diversity but also with change, innovation, teamwork, openness to new ideas, organizational flexibility, and creativity. The video comes complete with a leader's guide, including training designs on empowerment and diversity, seminar exercises and handouts, and a bibliography.

"Pigeonholed in the Land of Penguins" (11 minutes)

This charming animated video is the perfect addition to any diversity consultant's tool kit or training department's video library. Like this book, the video deals with the problem of stereotyping in organizations and explores diversity and team-work, diversity and creativity, and the importance of seeing beyond stereotypes to maximize the opportunity for everyone to contribute to his or her organization's success. The video comes complete with a leader's guide, which includes training designs, exercises and handouts, and a bibliography.

Books, Assessment Tools, and Training Materials

A Peacock in the Land of Penguins: A Tale of Diversity and Discovery

This is the book that started it all! The story of Perry the Peacock and his adventures in the Land of Penguins has reached the hearts and minds of readers everywhere. First published in 1995, and now available in twelve languages around the world, this corporate fable explores what it means to be different in a world that values conformity, stability, and tradition. The book includes a quiz to see if you are a Peacock in the Land of Penguins, as well as survival tips and strategies for birds of all types.

"Birds of Different Feathers Work Style Assessment"

Are you a hawk, an owl, a peacock, or a dove? This work style self-assessment helps you determine what kind of bird *you* are. Simple, quick, and easy to use, this self-assessment is enlightening and entertaining, as you see what kind of feathers you have, and learn how to work better with "birds" who are different from you. The instrument also includes a group assessment, so you can determine the prevalent work style of your department, team, or organization. It's perfect for individuals who seek self-understanding, as well as for training seminars on teamwork, diversity, communication, leadership, and creativity.

"Diversity Dialogue," audio program (80 minutes)

This is a new audio program featuring BJ Gallagher Hateley and Dr. Warren H. Schmidt discussing many different aspects of the complex issue of diversity. It is a lively, entertaining, and educational dialogue designed to give the listener an overview or "crash course" on diversity — both from a personal point of view and an organizational point of view. The audio program comes with a self-study and discussion guide.

"Diversity Workshop Facilitator's Guide"

This comprehensive manual includes guidelines for conducting effective diversity seminars, as well as step-by-step instructions on conducting employee surveys regarding diversity acceptance in the organization. It also includes a section on career coaching, emphasizing diversity and organizational "fit." The guide comes complete with several training designs, seminar handouts, classroom exercises, overhead transparency masters, and a thorough bibliography of books, videos, audiotapes, journal articles, and additional resources.

"The Peacock Profile: Assessing Individual Uniqueness and Organizational 'Fit'"

How well do you fit in your organization? This simple, clear, 25-question assessment clarifies the fit between individuals and their jobs and organizations. It includes discussion questions, tips and strategies for increasing job satisfaction, and action planning for individuals.

"The Penguin Index: Assessing Management Practices and Diversity Acceptance in Your Organization"

Do you work in the Land of Penguins or the Land of Opportunity? This 25-question instrument is designed to assess your organization's culture and management practices. Simple and easy to administer, it works well in training seminars or as an employee survey. It includes diversity strategies for management, as well as positive strategies employees can use to make a difference in their organization.

Diversity Merchandise

Bird Pens and Feathered Pens

A variety of pens are available. Pens with brightly colored feather plumes and the message "Show Your True Colors!" bring home the message of being true to oneself. Other pens include four different bird types (hawk, peacock, owl, and dove) inscribed with the words "Birds of Different Feathers CAN Flock Together!" These are the perfect complement to any of our diversity assessment tools. The most magnificent pens available are green dollar-sign pens inscribed with the message "Diver$ity Deliver$ Dividend$" and topped with wonderful peacock plumes.

"Celebrate Diversity!" Buttons

Colorful buttons show Perry the Peacock and a couple of his penguin buddies, with the message "Celebrate Diversity!" Fun and inexpensive, these buttons are perfect for seminars and conferences.

"Celebrate Diversity!" T-Shirts

Colorful T-shirts are silk-screened with one of the most popular images from the book *A Peacock in the Land of Penguins*, a gathering of many different birds under the banner of "E Pluribus Maximus" (Greatness from Many). The T-shirts are white, with six-color silk-screen design. These are available on an individual basis or as a volume purchase for seminars and conferences.

"Magic" Penguin and Peacock Coffee Mugs

These unusual coffee mugs show a row of penguins against a dark blue background. When you pour in hot liquid, the blue background magically turns transparent, revealing a glorious Perry the Peacock with the words "Show Your True Colors!" among his tail feathers. This is a practical, everyday reminder of the message of being valued for who you really are.

Penguin Stress Toys

These four-inch tall squeezie penguins are very popular with all our clients. Irresistably cute, they almost beg to have the stuffing squeezed out of them! Soft and flexible, they can stand up to endless squeezing and scrunching, as you use them to relieve the stresses of living in the Land of Penguins. Comes with hilarious instructions: "25 Ways to Use Your Penguin Stress Toy."

Seminars, Keynote Speeches, Workshops, and Consulting Services

Contact Barbara "BJ" Hateley and Warren H. Schmidt at:

Peacock Productions
701 Danforth Drive
Los Angeles, CA 90065

Phone: 323-227-6205
Fax: 323-227-0705
E-mail: PeacockHQ@aol.com
Web site: www.peacockproductions.com

ABOUT THE AUTHORS

Barbara "BJ" Hateley

BJ Hateley is an accomplished management consultant and workshop leader, as well as a popular public speaker, specializing in customer service, sales, motivation, communications skills, leadership skills, workforce diversity, sexual harassment, managing your boss, career development, and specialized programs for women. She is president of her own human resources training and consulting company, Peacock Productions, and has worked with many corporate clients as well as professional associations, nonprofit groups, and government agencies. Her clients include: DaimlerChrysler, Chevron, IBM, Nissan, Volkswagen, Southern California Edison, Baxter Health Care, Phoenix Newspapers Inc., American Lung Association, Planned Parenthood, City of Pasadena, U.S. Immigration & Naturalization Service, American Press Institute, Certified Grocers of California, among others. She is a much-in-demand keynote speaker, making frequent presentations at conferences and professional gatherings in the United States, Asia, Europe, and Latin America.

Ms. Hateley has worked in the training and adult education field for twenty years. Before starting her own business in 1991, she spent nearly five years as manager of training and development for the *Los Angeles Times*, where she had key responsibilities in the areas of high-potential leadership development, management assessment and development, workforce diversity, team building, recruitment and selection training, sales training, and customer relations. Prior to that, she was the director of staff training and professional development for the University of Southern California, where she directed numerous programs for both faculty and staff. She served as an adjunct faculty member at USC's Andrus Gerontology Center for ten years.

Ms. Hateley is a Phi Beta Kappa graduate of USC, having earned her bachelor's degree summa cum laude in the field of social psychology. She has completed the course work for a Ph.D. in Social Ethics, also at USC. She has published articles in *Human Resource Executive*, the *Los Angeles Times, Training* magazine, and *Training and Development Journal,* among others. Her first book was *Telling Your Story, Exploring Your Faith* (Chalice Press, 1985), on personal development through life history writing. Her recent book, *A Peacock in the Land of Penguins: A Tale of Diversity and Discovery* (Berrett-Koehler, second edition 1997), coauthored with Dr. Warren H. Schmidt, is currently published in twelve languages worldwide. Her most recent book (cowritten with Eric Harvey) is *Customer at the Crossroads: From Parable to Practice* (San Francisco: Berrett-Koehler, 2000).

She has served as a commissioner on the City of Los Angeles Quality and Productivity Commission and as a board member for the Los Angeles chapter of the American Society for Training and Development (ASTD). She is an active member of the National Association of Women Business Owners, the National Speakers Association, and PEN Center USA West.

Contact BJ Hateley at Peacock Productions, 701 Danforth Drive, Los Angeles, CA 90065; phone 323-227-6205, fax 323-227-0705, e-mail PeacockHQ@aol.com.

Warren H. Schmidt

Dr. Warren H. Schmidt, a professor emeritus at the University of Southern California and UCLA, is president of Chrysalis, Inc., a management training and consulting company. His teaching, writing, and consulting activities are designed to apply social science knowledge to the problems of managing and working in public and private organizations. He is a certified psychologist in California and a diplomate of the American Board of Professional Psychology.

Dr. Schmidt's writings include books, articles, and film scripts. One of his films, an animated version of his parable, *Is It Always Right to be Right?* (narrated by Orson Wells), won an Academy Award in 1971, and was named Training Film of the Decade by the U.S. Industrial Film Board in 1980. He has screen credits for more than ninety management and educational films, in which he has participated as writer, performer, or adviser. He is the coauthor of *The Race Without a Finish Line: America's Quest for Total Quality* as well as *TQManager* both with Jerome Finnigan of Xerox. He and Robert Tannenbaum coauthored a Harvard Business Review Classic on *How to Choose a Leadership Pattern,* which has sold over one million copies, and he has written and published numerous other professional articles on a wide range of management topics. His recent book *A Peacock in the Land of Penguins: A Tale of Diversity and Discovery,* was coauthored with Barbara "BJ" Hateley.

Dr. Schmidt has been a consultant to both public and private organizations and is a frequent speaker on executive programs throughout the United States and abroad. He is currently

Chairman of the World Heritage Foundation. He has served on the board of governors for the American Society for Training and Development (ASTD) and for several years chaired the Los Angeles County Economy and Efficiency Commission. He was a member of the City of Los Angeles Quality and Productivity Commission for seven years and served as its president in 1990-91. He currently serves on the professional advisory board for the Los Angeles Police Department.

Dr. Schmidt's education includes a bachelor's degree from Wayne State University, a master of divinity degree from Concordia Seminary in St. Louis, and an M.A. and Ph.D. in psychology from Washington University. After teaching psychology at the University of Missouri, Union College, and Springfield College, Dr. Schmidt held various faculty and administrative positions at UCLA, including director of the unified MBA program and dean of executive education in the graduate school of management. He joined the USC faculty in 1976 as professor of public administration and was awarded professor emeritus status in 1991.

Dr. Schmidt can be contacted at Chrysalis, Inc., 9238 Petit Avenue, North Hills, CA 91343. Phone: 818-892-3092, fax 818-892-6991.

Sam Weiss

Sam Weiss has been recognized as one of the preeminent directors in the animation industry for the past twenty-five years. In addition, he brings his unique artistic style to the illustration of books and other print materials, adding character and a charm all his own. He is a versatile artist, film director, musician, and all-around creative spirit.

Mr. Weiss has written and/or directed numerous business-oriented training videos, including *The Winds of Change, To Try Again and Succeed, That's Not My Problem, I Told Them Exactly How To Do It, The Race Without a Finish Line,* and *A Peacock in the Land of Penguins.* His most recent productions are *A Complaint Is a Gift* for Excellence in Training Corporation (ETC), *How in Hell Do They Manage?* for CRM Films, and *The Blame Game* for corVision Media.

The films he has directed have been honored all over the world. He received an Academy Award nomination for *The Legend of John Henry,* sung by Roberta Flack, and a Television Academy Emmy for *The Wrong Way Kid* (which included four adapted children's books). He has won the Gold Award of the Art Directors Club of New York, Outstanding Film of the Year at the London Film Festival, First Prize at the Zagreb International Film Festival, the Jack London Award, and numerous other awards and honors.

Mr. Weiss has worked on a number of cartoon series and children's shows. He was art director and designer on the *Mr. Magoo* and *Bullwinkle* shows. He produced and directed *Hot Wheels,* one of the hottest animated series of the late 1960s, as well as thirty-five *G.I. Joe's* for Marvel Productions. He was staff director at Bosustow Entertainment for eleven years, where he directed more than fifty films, including four CBS one-hour specials, which required the adaptation of over thirty children's books to animation.

During his career he has directed voice talents of the stature of Carol Burnett, Alan Arkin, James Earl Jones, Milton Berle, Rob Reiner, Mickey Rooney, Stan Freberg, Patrick Stewart, and many other notable actors and singers.

His education includes studies at the Rhode Island School of Design and the Art Center College of Design.

Sam Weiss can be contacted at Sam Weiss Productions, 401 Sycamore Road, Santa Monica, CA 90402. Phone and fax 310-459-8838.